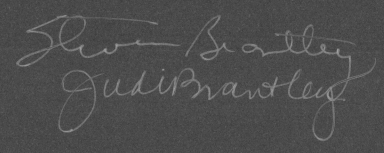

Given to:

By:

On:

For Molly, who looks for and finds the miracles of God.
For all God's children—the born, the unborn and the born again.   John 3:3
J.S.B. & T.S.B.

For the glory of God; for all to come to know Jesus Christ as their Lord and Savior.   John 3:16
For my husband, Chevis, who is a blessing from the Lord and for helping on pages 28, 29 and 31.
With special thanks to Elizabeth, Martha, Caity, Bobby, Michael, Meagan and Freddie who were my models.
C.M.C.

Then spake Jesus again unto them, saying, "I am the light of the world: he that followeth me
shall not walk in darkness, but shall have the light of life."   John 8:12

The Perfect Christmas Tree

Written by

Judi and Steven Brantley

Paintings by

Carol McDaniel-Clark

Spring House Books   Wadmalaw Island, South Carolina

The afternoon sun flooded through the windows. Warm, golden light splashed over the walls and floor. "Br-r-r!" Molly shivered as she changed into her warmest clothes and pulled on her favorite boots. She wore her farm boots everyday until this fall. She had started first grade. Now, they were reserved for stomping around on afternoons and weekends.

Molly felt nervous as she recalled her daddy's announcement on Thanksgiving Day. Her momma had smiled, winked, and nodded in approval as he spoke.

"Molly," her daddy said. "Remember, every year one of us chooses the Christmas tree." He raised his eyebrows and smiled. "And this year it's your time to choose the tree."

"Me?" she asked, putting her small hand over her heart. Her eyes widened with excitement—and a little fear. Everyone before her had chosen the perfect Christmas tree. Her heart had quickened then; even now, she felt it beating faster.

Jessica immediately leaned toward her little sister. "Molly, don't worry," Jessica said. "It's hard to explain. But, it's like the tree chooses and calls you! All you have to do is listen with your heart. And you'll know it's the *Perfect Tree*—the one you should choose."

Listen with my heart? This was a new concept for Molly. She found listening with her ears difficult at times. It seemed she was constantly in motion. Even when she was still, her mind raced with thoughts, questions, and ideas.

Molly loved mystery. The season of Christmas, she was learning, was wrapped in mystery. And today, she would be wrapped in a Christmas mystery of her own.

"Daddy, I'm just about ready," she called. Finally! She had finished her Saturday chores. All day her thoughts had been on choosing the perfect tree. And now, she didn't want any further delays.

"Okay, Miss Molly," her daddy called back. "The truck and I are ready whenever you are."

She loved being called Miss Molly. Her eyes alight with pride and her smile breaking into a laugh, Molly climbed into the old truck beside her daddy.

She looked out the frosty window. The late afternoon sun was still shining brightly, but the cold air and clouds circling overhead held the promise of snow.

The tree farm was only a few miles away. As the truck rattled to a stop at the grove of trees, Molly's heart started beating fast. *They all look so perfect!* Molly thought. *How will I ever be able to listen with my heart?*

Molly's mind whirled with questions. She watched the sun play hide-and-seek with the clouds. The clouds were hanging low on the horizon like gray, over-stuffed pillows. "Daddy, do you think it's going to snow again?"

They opened the doors of the truck and made their exit before he answered.

"Yes, as a matter of fact, I requested it especially for you."

Molly gave him one of her looks, which made him chuckle. "No, I mean really, Daddy?" she complained. However, Molly knew her daddy often made requests for others—he was a minister.

"Actually," he said as he put his hand in midair, "it's beginning to snow now."

Looking up, she saw the sun peek through again.
But he was right—floating like feathers, lacy snowflakes
were drifting into Molly's uplifted hands.

Crunch. Crunch. Crunch. Their boots crushed the crusty snow as they walked. The grove of towering trees, dressed in forest green tuxedos and draped with white wool mantles, stood as watchmen for a winter journey. It was the perfect stage for Molly's drama.

"Daddy, do you think we'll see a deer?" Molly questioned. She was always full of expectation.

"We might. Who knows? We might see a very special deer," he said. "Because Christmas is certainly a special season, filled with miracles and mystery. Now, let's hurry and find the tree before darkness comes."

Before long, the snow was falling heavily. A few rays of the setting sun came from behind the clouds and fell on the fresh snowflakes covering the trees. The light sparkled and glistened, as if the Christmas lights were already in place. Molly's eyes and heart captured it all. Another question rang through Molly's head. "Daddy, why do we put up a Christmas tree?"

"Well," he began carefully. Before he could finish, a neighbor asked him a question about his sermon on Sunday. And naturally, his favorite subjects were God's word and his family. With enthusiasm, he began his explanation and before he knew it 10 minutes were gone. Abruptly, aware of how long he had been talking, he looked around and realized Molly had slipped away.

"Molly! Molly!" he called. But there was no answer.

Full of excitement, Molly rushed ahead without him, going deeper and deeper into the grove of trees. Sometimes she ran. Sometimes she walked. Making circles around and around, she wove in and out of trees. She examined each one and gave it a chance to call to her.

Molly's attention was entirely on the trees. She was unaware of how far she was going; how the time was slipping away; how the evening light was fading; and how her daddy was frantically calling her name.

Molly stopped. Her heart was beating fast. Could this be the one? Bending her head back, she looked to the very top of the tree. As she began walking around the tree, it happened. In her heart, Molly heard the tree call. She was chosen. This was the perfect tree! None of the other trees had touched her heart like this. And she had considered a lot of them.

Molly's mystery grew. Everything about this tree was perfect. The color was a deep, pure evergreen. The branches reached out like arms that said, "Welcome!" And the trunk—her daddy had reminded her to check for straightness—was strong and straight. Her search was over.

Molly sat down under the tree to rest and to wait until her daddy could catch up. It was almost dark. She was sure he would be coming soon.

The crystal flakes of falling snow reflected the radiant light of a full moon peeking through the breaking clouds. Molly, watching the moonbeam shimmer on snow-covered branches of first one tree, and then another, missed seeing Snowflake appear. Suddenly, she sensed she was not alone.

The most beautiful deer she had ever seen stood to the side of the tree. The deer's face and neck were a creamed-coffee brown. The rest of her coat was so milky that she seemed to glow in the moonlight. Molly blinked and thought, *I must be dreaming*. She blinked again. The deer was still there! In a soft, quiet voice, knowing how timid deer are, Molly said, "Hello." She was surprised that, as she spoke, the deer did not bolt away. "Hello," Molly repeated. "What's your name?"

Moving closer, the deer greeted Molly with a graceful bow. She folded her right leg under, and on an extended left leg, she lowered her head and body.

Then, the deer said, "My name is Snowflake. I have been sent to wait with you and tell you the Christmas tree story." And she lay down beside Molly, beneath the branches of the perfect tree.

Unlike the peace surrounding Snowflake and Molly, chaos was brewing at the start of the grove. When her daddy realized Molly had gone into the trees without him, he began running and calling for her. But Molly, so deep in the wood, could not hear him. Now, Molly's daddy and the townspeople were gathering to begin a search for her.

The owner of the grove cut into the confusion. "Everyone. Please. Listen." His voice was mighty, yet kind. "Although the grove seems enormous and darkness has come, we are not without hope. I have divided the grove into sections. Each one of you will have a section to search. She will be found. Those of you who need light, come and fill your lanterns with oil."

Many came and filled their lanterns while the owner continued his directions. "The ones who have the farthest to go will start first, then the next will begin, and the next, until the light from the lanterns joins, leaving the darkness powerless. Any questions?" No one spoke.

"Go then. And Godspeed."

The owner's calm spread peace over them like a blanket; without hesitation, everyone crowded into the trees, casting light from upheld lanterns into the thick darkness. Molly's daddy led the people.

Deep in the forest, beneath the branches of the perfect tree, Snowflake began the Christmas tree story. "Molly, do you know where Germany is?"

Molly shook her head slowly and answered. "Not really. I mean, I know it's in Europe."

"And you know Europe is a long way from Virginia, right?"

Molly's face brightened. "Oh, yes, I know that."

"Germany is where the Christmas tree story starts. Do you know what a symbol is?"

Molly tried to concentrate on what Snowflake was saying and the questions she was asking. But her mind took her back to the night Jesus was born.

She remembered a legend of how the animals had spoken the language of humans. *Was the mystery of that night being repeated?*

"What did you ask me?"
Molly questioned, realizing she had
been lost for a moment in another time.

"Do you know what a symbol is?"

"Yes! It's something that reminds us of something else," Molly said proudly.

"Right! The Christmas tree is a symbol. Actually, it's a combination of two symbols. Long ago, many years after Jesus was born, the people of Germany started a tradition. Do you know what a tradition is?"

"Yes, I know that too," Molly replied. "It's when something is done over and over from one year to the next or from one generation to the next. Our family started a tradition. Each year one of us chooses the tree—or is chosen by the tree," she added quietly.

"Yes, and symbols are often used in traditions and celebrations," Snowflake said. "On December 24th, the people of Germany celebrated two separate events. They celebrated Adam and Eve's Day by cutting down an evergreen tree and decorating it with apples. The tree symbolized the Paradise Tree from the Garden of Eden, and the apples symbolized man's sin. They also celebrated the birth of Jesus, the light of the world, by using a wooden pyramid, which held lighted candles. The candle pyramid was called a lichtstock. These two symbols were eventually combined, and people started putting up the Christmas tree. The Christmas tree symbolizes the tree of life—everlasting life—the promise of Christmas. The lights on the tree symbolize Jesus, the light of the world, through whom the promise comes."

Molly looked up at the tree and said,
"You know what else it looks like? It
looks like an arrow pointing to heaven, while it
touches the earth." She surprised herself with the
truth in what she said and continued. "That's exactly what Jesus did while
He was here. He was always pointing us to heaven while He touched the earth."
It was the last thing Molly remembered saying to Snowflake before she fell asleep.

Piercing the darkness with
the light from his lantern,
Molly's daddy pressed
on. He chose one
of the farthest
sections to
search.
In choosing,
he took the advice
Jessica had offered Molly:
he listened with his heart.
He quickened his pace as he
thought of his child, lost in the
dark and the cold. He shivered.
She was so little against the darkness.

Something was moving just ahead of him. He stopped. His heart was beating fast. What was that in front of him? His vision was blurred from the snowflakes melting on his face. He blinked. Then he saw the tree. "What a perfect tree!" he said aloud. The very top seemed to point into the heavens, while the beautiful branches touched the earth.

"Molly," he whispered, seeing her curled beneath the tree. The branches covered her small body and protected her from the blinding snow.

He kneeled. Tenderly, he picked her
up as she sleepily said, "Daddy, the perfect tree found me. This is the one!"

    "Yes, Molly," he said, speaking slowly, his voice breaking and his eyes
brimming with tears. "This is the perfect tree." The wondrous perfection of the tree
filled him with awe. He realized the perfect tree had saved his child. The tears,
which filled his eyes to overflowing, quietly slipped down his cheeks.

    Molly broke the silence. "Daddy, did you see Snowflake?"

    "Who?"

    "Snowflake. The white deer who came after the tree found me. She said she was
sent to wait with me and tell me the Christmas tree story," Molly said, without taking
a breath. "She kept me warm."

Smiling, he turned in the direction Molly was pointing.

Suddenly, he saw her. She was stately, with her creamed-coffee brown face and neck and glowing, milky coat. Snowflake is what he had seen moving, just before he saw the perfect tree. She was his messenger to Molly. He was greeted in the same fashion Molly had witnessed, with a graceful bow. He blinked, and the deer was gone. And he, too, was wrapped in another mystery of Christmas.

Suffer the little children to come unto me, and forbid them not: for of such is the kingdom of God.   Mark 10:14

Published by
Spring House Books
Wadmalaw Island, South Carolina

Edited by: Pringle Franklin   Mt. Pleasant, South Carolina

Acknowledgments
We give special thanks to Pringle Franklin for her assistance and Biblical insights.
She helped to make our book better.
And to Carol McDaniel-Clark for her godly interpretation and renderings of the paintings for *The Perfect
Christmas Tree.*
And to Jon Verdi for the impressive jacket cover script and the art of the cross.
And to all those who have faithfully covered this project in prayer.

First Printing 2000

Scripture quoted is from THE HOLY BIBLE, The Authorized King James Version.

Typesetting and Formatting by: Jon Verdi Graphic Design.

Printed in Hong Kong by C & C Offset Printing Company, Ltd.

Library of Congress Catalog Card Number: 00-90588

ISBN 1-892570-05-X

10 9 8 7 6 5 4 3 2 1